THIS WALKER BOOK BELONGS TO:

To Caz and Helen, Clare and Julia, Amelia, Liz and Ben • with my love and thanks for all your help H.C.

First published 1995 by Walker Books Ltd
87 Vauxhall Walk, London SE11 5HJ

This edition published 1999

2 4 6 8 10 9 7 5 3 1

© 1995 Helen Craig

The right of Helen Craig to be identified as author
of this work has been asserted by her in accordance with
the Copyright, Designs and Patents Act 1988.

This book has been typeset in Garamond.

Printed in Singapore

British Library Cataloguing in Publication Data
A catalogue record for this book is
available from the British Library.

ISBN 0-7445-6778-5 (hb)
ISBN 0-7445-7224-X (pb)

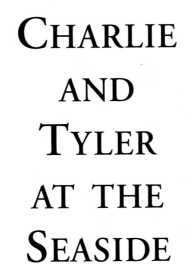

CHARLIE
AND
TYLER
AT THE
SEASIDE

HELEN CRAIG

WALKER BOOKS
AND SUBSIDIARIES
LONDON • BOSTON • SYDNEY

One warm sunny day, Charlie the country mouse was sitting on the porch of his comfortable home in the hedgerow. He was reading a letter from his cousin Tyler the town mouse. This is what it said:

Dear Charlie,
   How's life with you?
   As dull as ever, I expect.
   Well, now's your chance to do something exciting. Meet me tomorrow at the old oak tree an hour before sunrise for A DAY AT THE SEASIDE!
                    love, Tyler

"Oh dear!" said Charlie. "I don't want to do something exciting. I'm quite happy here." But next morning he got up while it was still dark, shouldered his old satchel and set off all the same.

Tyler was waiting for him by the oak tree, rigged out in a sailor's jersey and a sea captain's hat.
"Ahoy there!" he called. "Here comes Mrs Pigeon. She's going to give us a lift."

The sun was just rising as Mrs
Pigeon set Charlie and Tyler down
on the seashore.
"Have a lovely day," she said. "And
don't forget, meet me on the cliff top
at sunset and I'll take you home."

They looked around them. Out of the mist loomed a big shape.
"It's a motorboat!" said Tyler. "Let's go for a trip. I'll be captain
because I know about boats. Welcome aboard, Able-seaman Charlie."

Tyler looked around for the
controls, but he couldn't find any.
"Ah!" he said. "Just a small setback.
Let's wait until the mist clears."
So the two little mice settled down
in the cabin for a snooze.

They were woken by a loud
whirring noise.
"What's happening?" squeaked Charlie.
Waves were flashing past the windows.

"We're at sea – I think,"
said Tyler as the boat
lurched one way and
then the other.

"Can't you stop it?" Charlie
wailed. "You're captain."
But Captain Tyler had no
idea *what* to do.

The two mice scrambled on deck and hung on tight. The boat was

speeding madly all by itself, backwards and forwards across the water.

They were frightened for their lives.

At last the boat hurtled towards
the shore and hit a rock.
Charlie and Tyler were catapulted
into the air and landed – SPLASH!
– in a shallow pool.
"Oh dear, oh dear," said Charlie.

But Tyler picked himself
up and looked around.

"Let's go beachcombing," he said.
"What's beachcombing?" asked Charlie.
"It's looking for treasure and useful things in the sand," Tyler replied, marching off.

He soon found a little sword that had once belonged to a toy soldier, and a metal badge that made a perfect shield.

Charlie found a parasol and a little bell on a chain. "This will be just right for my front door," he said. He was beginning to enjoy himself. They set off again, their bags laden with treasure.

At last they found themselves under the pier.

"Hey, we can have some fun up there!" said Tyler. "It's only a little climb."

Charlie looked up with a sinking heart. But a great big dog was lolloping towards them. He had no choice but to follow.

Way down below, the waves splashed and the dog barked. "This is scary," said Charlie. "Nonsense!" said Tyler.

Underneath the floorboards of the pier they found a hole and squeezed through into a very strange place.

"Oh, Tyler!" said Charlie. "What HAVE you got us into now?"

They climbed on and up into a dimly-lit room full of shadowy figures. "Where can we be?" whispered Charlie. All of a sudden lights came on, a curtain went up and music began to play. They were in a toy theatre!

With a whirring of the cogwheels below, the little figures began to move in time to the music. Tyler and

Charlie pretended they were part of the show, but too late – they'd been spotted. It was time for a quick exit.

"Phew!" puffed Tyler. "I'm hungry after all that. Let's find some food."

They had sausages, crisps, popcorn and a nice piece of toffee-apple...

And they did very well when it came to ice-cream.

They visited the aquarium
and the hall of mirrors.
All too soon it was time
to go and meet Mrs Pigeon.

Up on the cliff they sat
and watched the boats
out at sea. Charlie liked
it. It was almost as
peaceful as his home
in the hedgerow.

Then a terrible thing happened.

A huge seabird swooped down and grabbed Tyler in its claws.

"Help! Help!" he squeaked. Charlie watched in horror as the great bird carried Tyler far away.

Charlie began to cry. His eyes were so full of tears that he didn't see the bird turn in a circle and head back to her home under the cliff.

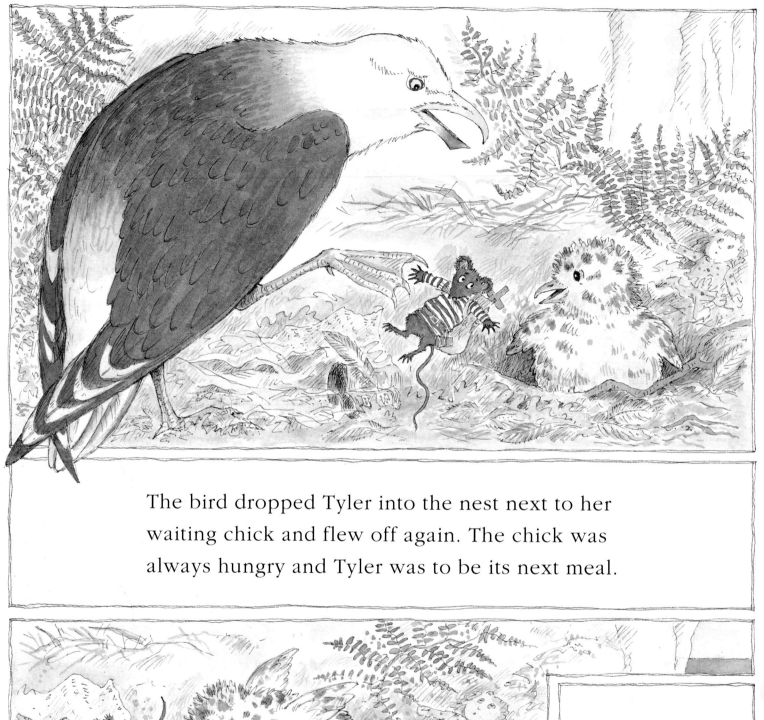

The bird dropped Tyler into the nest next to her waiting chick and flew off again. The chick was always hungry and Tyler was to be its next meal.

The chick moved closer to Tyler.

It gave him a peck.

Tyler was furious and drew his sword.

"Take that!"
he shouted.
"Ow!" squawked
the chick.

The awful noise they
made floated up to Charlie,
alone and sad on the cliff top.
He crept to the edge and
peeped over. He couldn't
believe his eyes.

"Hang on, Tyler!" he shouted. "I'm coming!" He started off down the cliff without a thought for the dangers below, tumbling, bouncing and sliding until he landed in a small bush just above the nest.

Quickly he pulled the little bell from his satchel
and lowered it down above Tyler's head.
"Grab hold and I'll pull you up," he shouted.

Tyler swung dangerously
over the sea. Charlie pulled
as hard as he could.

The chick squawked, but
by the time the mother bird
came back, Tyler was gone.

Charlie and Tyler scrambled
to the top of the cliff where
Mrs Pigeon found them later,
lying exhausted under some
large leaves.
"You poor things!" she cooed.
"You do look tired. Climb in
the postbag and I'll fly
you home."

The two mice took a last
look at the seaside. It all
seemed so peaceful from
the air.
"Charlie, you're a hero," said
Tyler. "You saved my life."

It was night when Mrs
Pigeon put them down
by the hedgerow.
"Goodbye and thanks,"
they called.

Safe and sound at Charlie's home, they sat on the porch
and talked over all that had happened.
"What a fine adventure we had!" said Tyler. Charlie wasn't so
sure. However, on one thing they did agree – they had both
been terribly, terribly BRAVE!

MORE WALKER PAPERBACKS
For You to Enjoy

THE TOWN MOUSE AND THE COUNTRY MOUSE
by Helen Craig

What happens when a town mouse visits a country mouse?
What happens when a country mouse visits a town mouse?
All is revealed in Helen Craig's lively retelling of Aesop's best-loved fable,
which was shortlisted for the Smarties Book Prize.

"Helen Craig's spirited retelling … is the best version of this
old favourite for many years." *The Economist*

0-7445-7223-1   £4.99

THE VERY BEST OF AESOP'S FABLES
by Margaret Clark/Charlotte Voake

Shortlisted for the Kurt Maschler Award, this is an entertaining selection of
eleven of the most popular of Aesop's classic tales – without the morals.

"Bright as new paint… Clear, snappy and sharp, yet retains all the elegance and point of the originals.
Delicately illustrated by the inimitable Charlotte Voake." *The Sunday Times*

0-7445-3149-7   £5.99

MARY MARY
by Sarah Hayes/Helen Craig

Formerly on the list of texts to be used in conjunction with the
Standard Assessment Tasks of the National Curriculum (Key Stage 2, Level 1 – 2),
this is the original tale of a shambolic giant and the small girl who sorts him out.

"This fairy tale has a friendly giant and an intrepid heroine,
two excellent ingredients for a winning story." *Child Education*

0-7445-2062-2   £4.99